Whisker Haven
TALES
with the
palace pets

Berry's Sweet Surprise

By Apple Jordan

Illustrated by Sue DiCicco
and Vivien Wu

 A GOLDEN BOOK • NEW YORK

randomhousekids.com
ISBN 978-0-7364-3444-7 (trade) — ISBN 978-0-7364-3445-4 (ebook)
Printed in the United States of America
10 9 8 7 6 5 4 3 2 1

It was a perfect spring day. The sun was shining. The birds were singing. The flowers were starting to bloom. Snow White's pet bunny, Berry, was hopping through the forest looking for her favorite treat—the first ripe berries of the season.

At last Berry came upon a berry patch. It was filled with berries as far as the eye could see. The bunny was so excited!

As Berry nibbled her way through the berry patch, she stumbled upon something under a huckleberry bush. It was round and white and hard. It was an **egg**!

Berry knew that eggs need to be kept warm. The furry bunny sat on the egg, wondering what type of bird was inside. She was excited to meet it!

So Berry **waited** . . .

and **waited** . . .

and **waited** . . .

until . . .

TAP! TAP! CRICK! CRAAAACK!

The egg started to hatch! Within moments, a baby duckling waddled his way out of the eggshell.

The duckling blinked in the morning sunshine. He
sniffed the fresh spring air. Then he walked straight up
to Berry and nuzzled his beak in the bunny's soft fur.

Berry immediately fell in love with the duckling. "I
promise to take good care of you forever," she told him.

"I bet you're hungry," Berry said. "I wonder what you like to eat."

Berry looked around for the perfect food. But she didn't have to worry—the little duckling was busy snacking on all of the delicious berries in the berry patch!

"Why, you like berries—just like me!" Berry cried with delight.

"I don't know much about waddling," said Berry, "but I can show you how to hop." Berry hop, hop, hopped across the grass.

The little duckling watched Berry. Then he hopped with his two webbed feet.

Hop, hop, hop!

"You're great at hopping," said Berry. "Just like me!"

Before Berry could think of what to do next, the little duckling hopped away.

"Where are you going?" Berry called, hopping after him.

The little duckling led Berry to the riverbank.

"Of course! You want to swim!" said Berry. "Well, bunnies aren't good swimmers, but I know ducks are. I'll stand here on the bank and watch you."

The little duckling bravely jumped into the river and splashed around happily. Berry was proud.

After the duckling was done swimming, Berry
suggested a game of hide-and-seek. "You hide, little
duckling, and I'll find you," Berry said.

Berry closed her eyes and began to count. "One,
two, three . . ."

The duckling hopped away to hide.

". . . eighteen, nineteen, twenty. Ready or not, here
I come!" Berry went in search of her little friend.

Berry hopped through the forest, looking behind every tree and under every berry bush.

She finally found the little duckling hiding beneath a plant.

"You're a very good hider, little duckling!" said Berry.

After all that hopping and swimming and playing, the duckling became tired.

"It's time for you to take a nap," said Berry. She made a comfortable nest out of grass and her own soft bunny fur. The duckling climbed in and fell fast asleep.

"I know we will be friends forever," Berry whispered to the duckling as she nestled in and **dozed** off.

When Berry woke up, she was alone in the nest. "Now, where did that little duckling go?" she said. "Maybe he's hiding again."

Berry hopped through the forest looking for her fuzzy friend.

She looked
behind every
pine tree.

She looked in
every **berry** bush.

She looked under every plant.

But the little duckling was nowhere to be found. Berry
was getting nervous.

"Come out, little duckling, wherever you are!" she cried.

Just then, Berry heard a splash at the river.
"Wait for me!" cried Berry, hopping as fast as she could.
But before she could get there, the little duckling
jumped in, webbed feet first.

When Berry reached the riverbank, she looked through the reeds and saw seven little ducklings and a mama duck! The little duckling had found his family!

Berry watched as her *fuzzy* friend happily floated down the river, following his family. Berry was glad he had found his mama, but she missed him.

Berry went back to the berry patch. The berries didn't taste as sweet now that her friend was gone. Then she heard a noise.

Quack! Quack! Quack!

"Little duckling! You came back!" cried Berry.

The little duckling's mother and six brothers and sisters had come, too. Mama Duck was carrying a branch of berries in her bill.

"These are for you," she said, placing the branch next to Berry's feet. "Thank you for taking such good care of my little duckling. His egg had rolled away from the nest and I couldn't find it anywhere. He is so lucky you found him."

"No," said Berry. "*I'm* lucky I found him." She gave the little duckling a big hug goodbye.

Berry watched happily as Mama Duck and her
ducklings headed back to the river. Last in line was
Berry's little duckling friend.